A ROOKIE READER®

SNEAKY PETE

By Rita Milios

Illustrations by Clovis Martin

Prepared under the direction of Robert Hillerich, Ph.D.

CHILDRENS PRESS®
CHICAGO

Library of Congress Cataloging-in-Publication Data

Milios, Rita.
   Sneaky Pete / by Rita Milios ; illustrated by Clovis
Martin.
      p. cm. — (A Rookie reader)
   Summary: Sneaky Pete proves why he's the
champion of Hide and Seek.
   ISBN 0-516-02092-7
   [1. Hide-and-seek—Fiction. 2. Stories in rhyme.]
I. Martin, Clovis, ill. II. Title. III. Series.
PZ8.3.M59 Sn 1989
[E]—dc20   89-34666
                                               CIP
                                              AC

Sneaky Pete sneaks around.

People look, but he's never found.

Sister looks behind a chair.
Sneaky Pete is not there.

Mother looks across the lawn.

Pete was here, but now he's gone.

Dad looks under the bed.

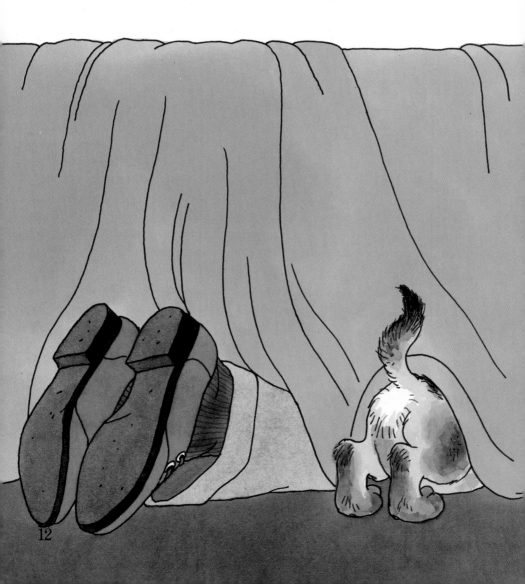

"He's not here," Daddy said.

14

Baby sister finds a clue.

Sneaky Pete has lost a shoe.

He can't get far. Where did he go?

Sneaky Pete, why don't you show?

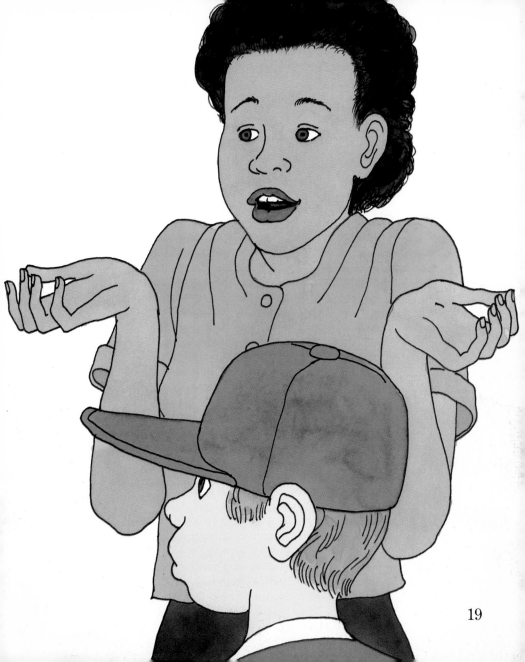

Looking here, looking there,
Looking, looking everywhere.

Sneaky Pete sneaks around.

People look, but he's never found.

Sneaky Pete, quick on his feet.

The champion of Hide and Seek!

WORD LIST

a	everywhere	lawn	seek
across	far	look	shoe
and	feet	looking	show
around	finds	looks	sister
baby	found	lost	sneaks
bed	get	mother	sneaky
behind	go	never	the
but	gone	not	there
can't	has	now	under
champion	he	of	was
clue	he's	on	where
dad	here	people	why
daddy	hide	Pete	you
did	his	quick	
don't	is	said	

About the Author

Rita Milios lives in Toledo, Ohio, with her husband and two grade-school children. She is a freelance writer and instructor in the Continuing Education department at Toldeo University. She has published numerous articles in magazines including *McCall's*, *Lady's Circle*, and *The Writer*. She is currently working on her first adult book. Mrs. Milios is the author of *Sleeping and Dreaming* in the New True Book series. She has written two other Rookie Readers: *I Am* and *Bears, Bears, Everywhere*.

About the Artist

Clovis Martin has enjoyed a varied career as an art teacher, art director, and freelance illustrator. He has designed and illustrated a variety of reading, educational, and other products for children. A graduate of The Cleveland Institute of Art, he resides with his wife and two children in Cleveland Heights, Ohio.